This edition published by Parragon Books Ltd in 2016

Parragon Books Ltd
Chartist House
15–17 Trim Street
Bath BA1 1HA, UK
www.parragon.com

Copyright © 2016 Disney/Pixar

All rights reserved. No part of this publication may be reproduced, stored in a retrieval system or transmitted, in any form or by any means, electronic, mechanical, photocopying, recording or otherwise, without the prior permission of the copyright holder.

ISBN 978-1-4748-2767-6

Printed in China

Disney · PIXAR
Finding NEMO

Parragon

Bath • New York • Cologne • Melbourne • Delhi
Hong Kong • Shenzhen • Singapore • Amsterdam

Marlin the clownfish lived happily with his wife on the Great Barrier Reef. But one awful day, a Barracuda attacked the clownfish. Poor Marlin lost his wife and all but one of the eggs, which he named Nemo.

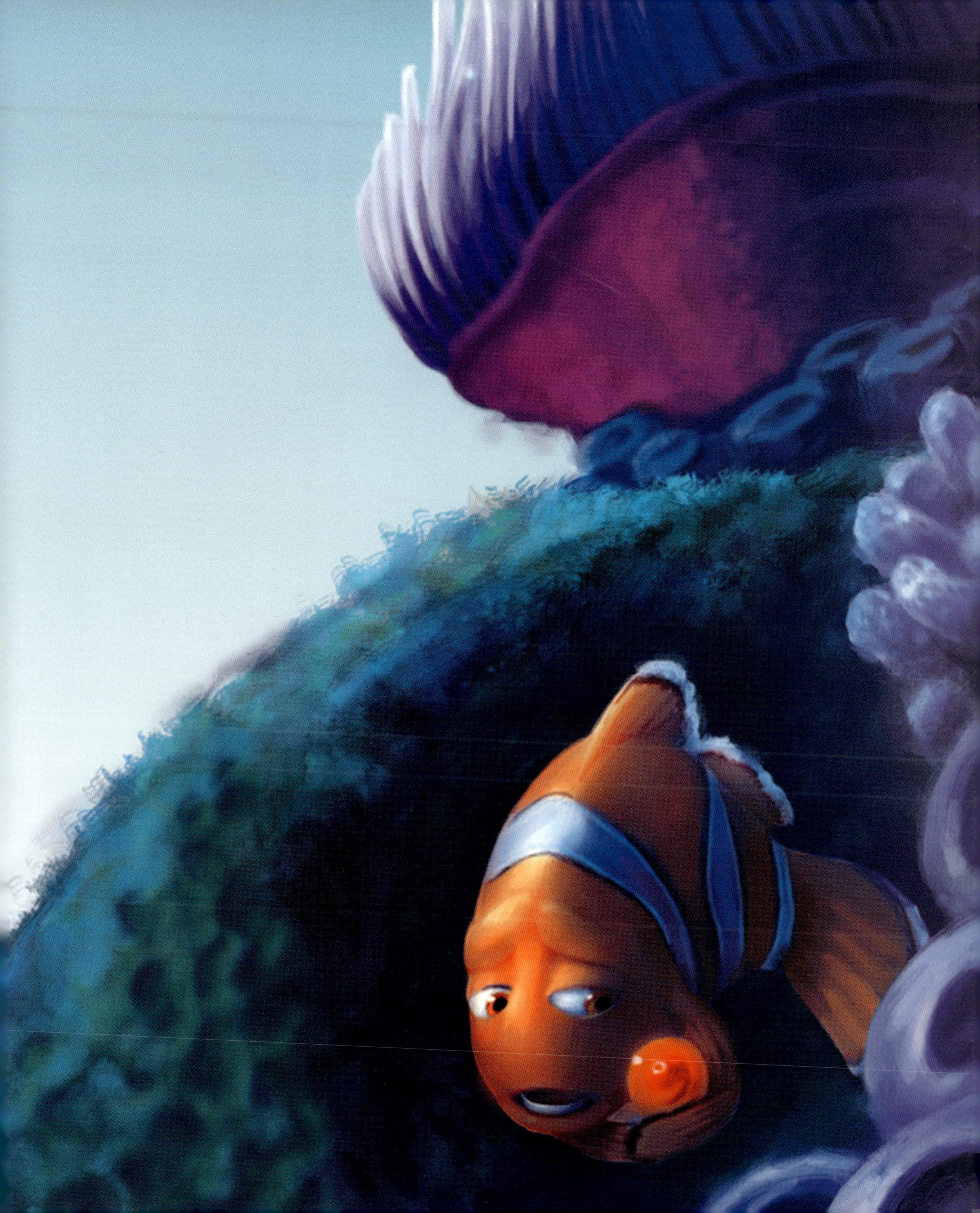

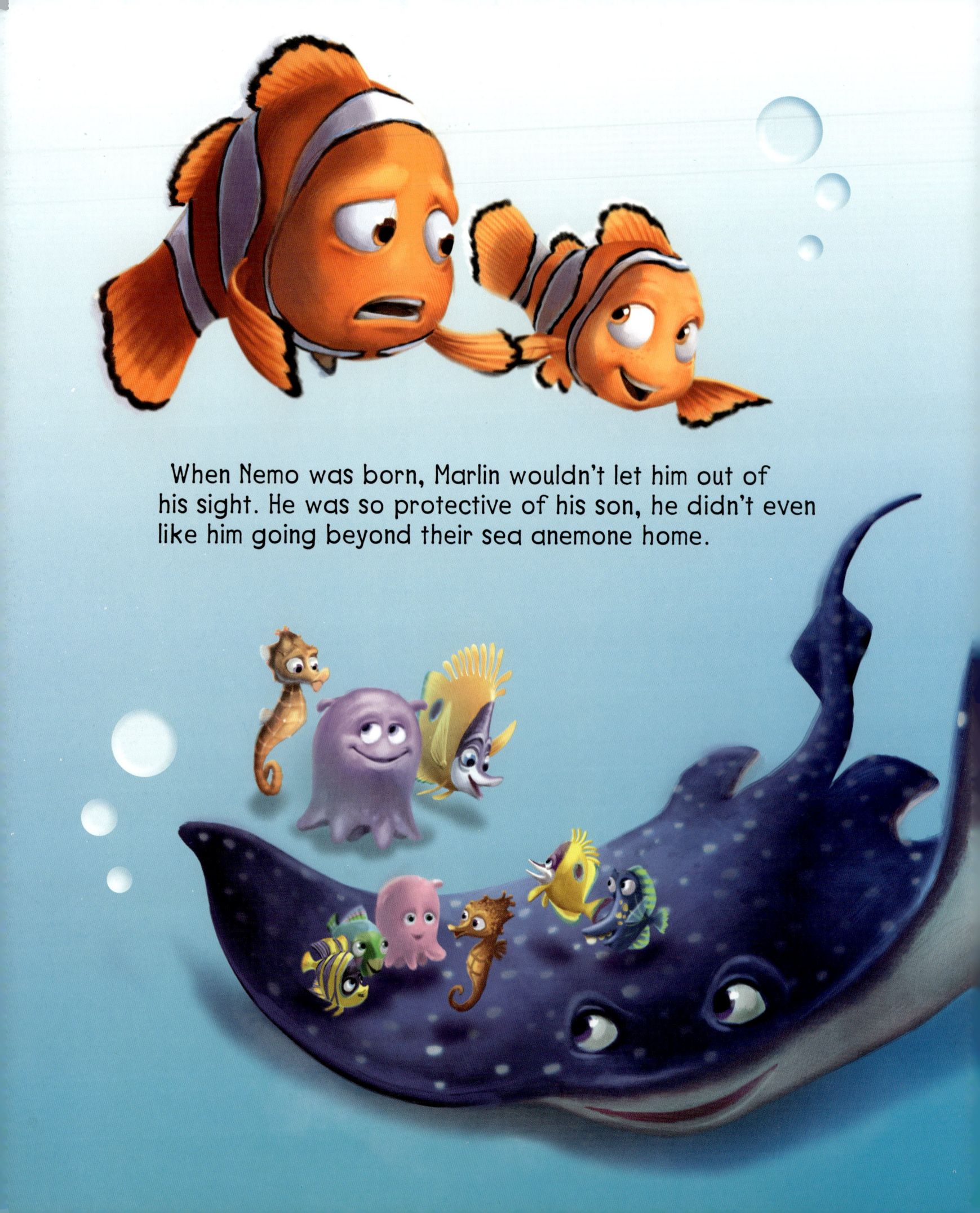

When Nemo was born, Marlin wouldn't let him out of his sight. He was so protective of his son, he didn't even like him going beyond their sea anemone home.

Finally, it was time for Nemo's first day of school. Nemo was ready for adventure! His new friends dared him to swim out into the open sea. Nemo felt nervous, so he didn't swim very far.

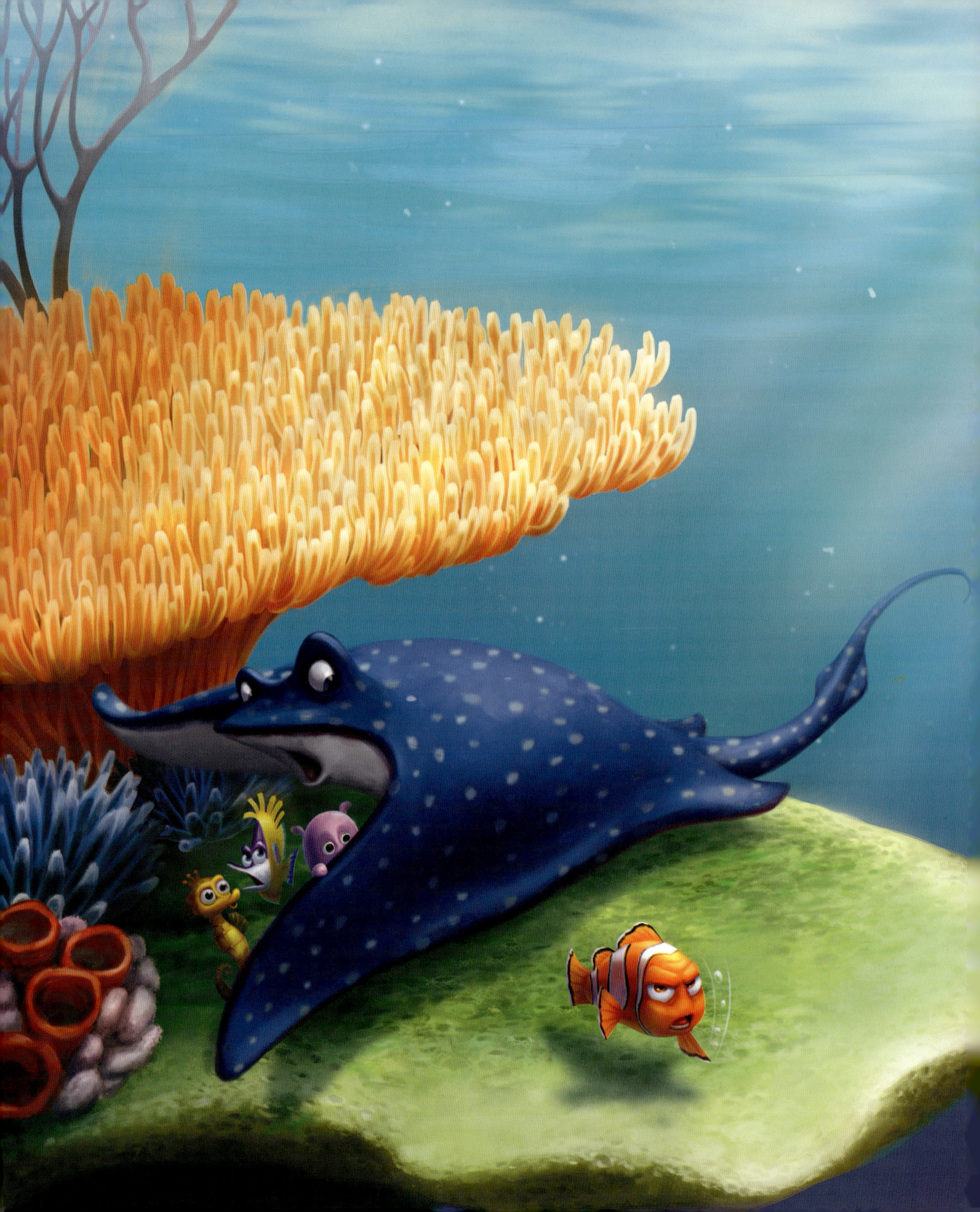

When Marlin found out what had happened, he shouted at Nemo. 'You think you can do these things but you just can't!' he said.

Nemo was cross with his dad. He swam off in a huff – right into the path of a diver!

'Daddy! Help me!' Nemo screamed, as the diver caught him in a net. Horrified, Marlin raced after the diver's boat, but it was too late. It had already disappeared!

Marlin asked everyone he could find if they'd seen a boat. 'Follow me!' said a bright blue tang fish called Dory. But Dory had a very bad memory. One minute later, she couldn't remember why Marlin was following her.
'Will you quit it?' she asked.

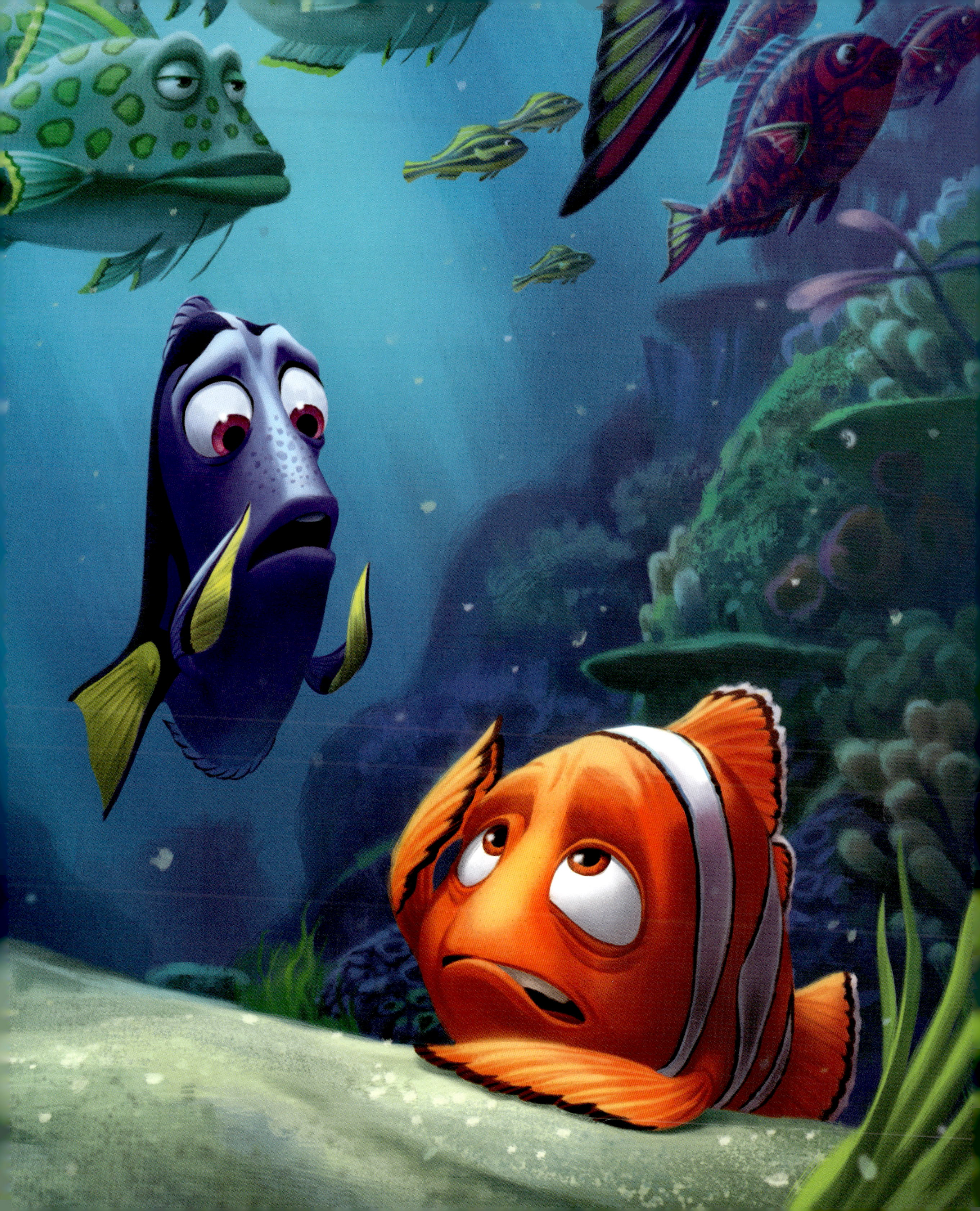

Just then, Marlin and Dory ran into a huge shark called Bruce. Luckily, he was friendly so he didn't eat them!

'Look!' said Marlin, suddenly. He had spotted a diver's mask. It must have fallen off the diver's boat.

Maybe it was a clue that could help them find Nemo!

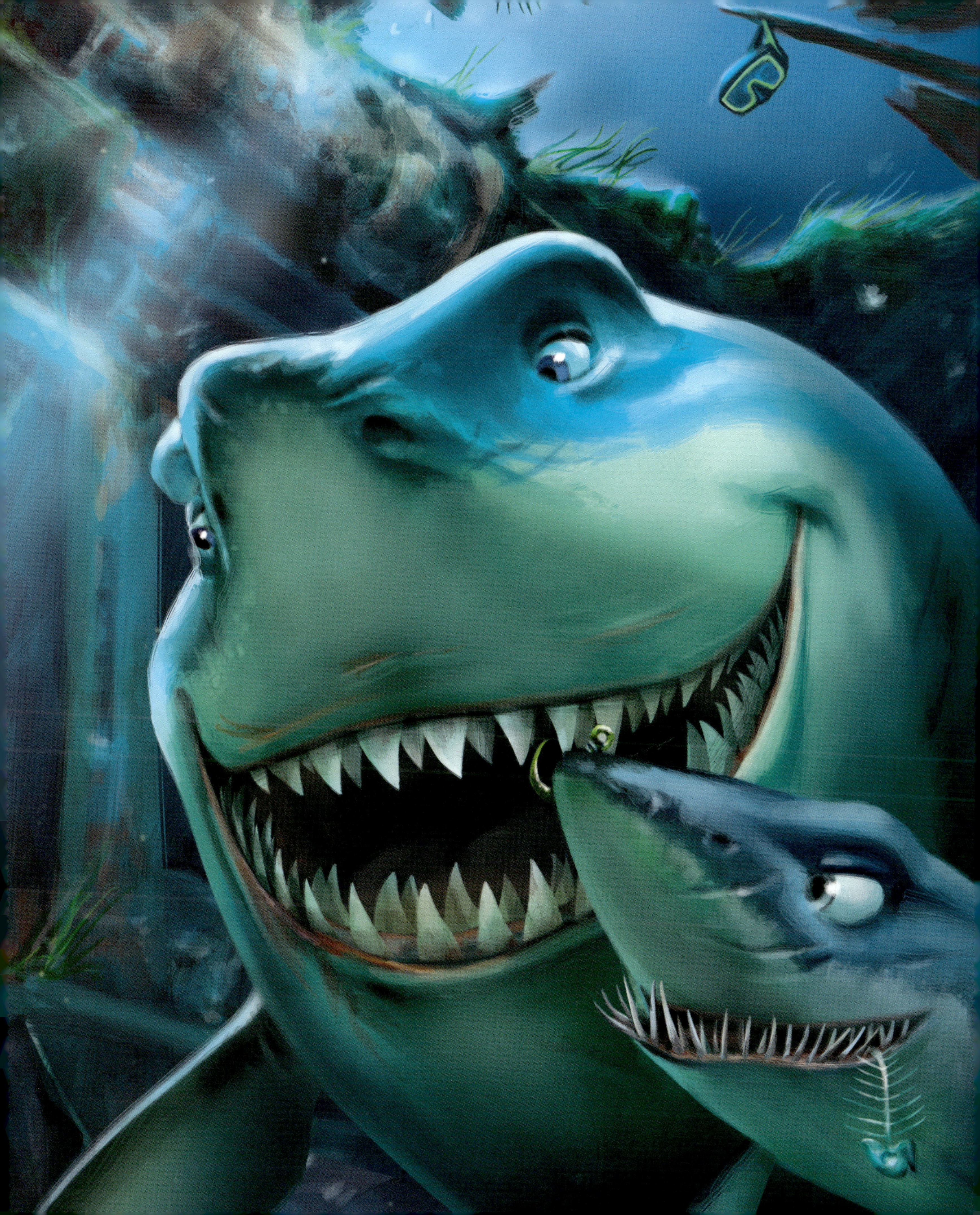

Meanwhile, Nemo had been taken to a dentist's fish tank in Sydney, Australia. He made friends with the other fish, who told him he was going to be a present for Darla, the dentist's niece. The fish warned Nemo that Darla was a 'fish killer'!

That night, Nemo's new friends held a welcoming ceremony for him. Nemo had to swim through the RING OF FIRE!

But the ring was really just a stream of bubbles! The fish gave brave little Nemo a new name — Shark Bait.

Out in the ocean, Marlin and Dory were suddenly attacked by an anglerfish. But Marlin cleverly used the diver's mask to trap their scary attacker.

Then Dory spotted an address on the mask strap. 'P. Sherman, 42 Wallaby Way, Sydney.'

Marlin was anxious to find Nemo quickly so he suggested that he carry on alone. Thinking that Marlin didn't like her, Dory started to cry. Thankfully a passing school of moonfish were able to cheer her up with their clever impressions!

The moonfish gave Marlin and Dory directions to Sydney. Dory insisted on helping her friend and the pair swam on together, accidentally ending up in a deep trench filled with lots of jellyfish!

The jellyfish started stinging poor Marlin and Dory! They needed help! Luckily, some sea turtles came swimming past and rescued them.

'Takin' on the jellies – awesome!' said Crush, a surfer turtle. He was impressed with Marlin and Dory's bravery.

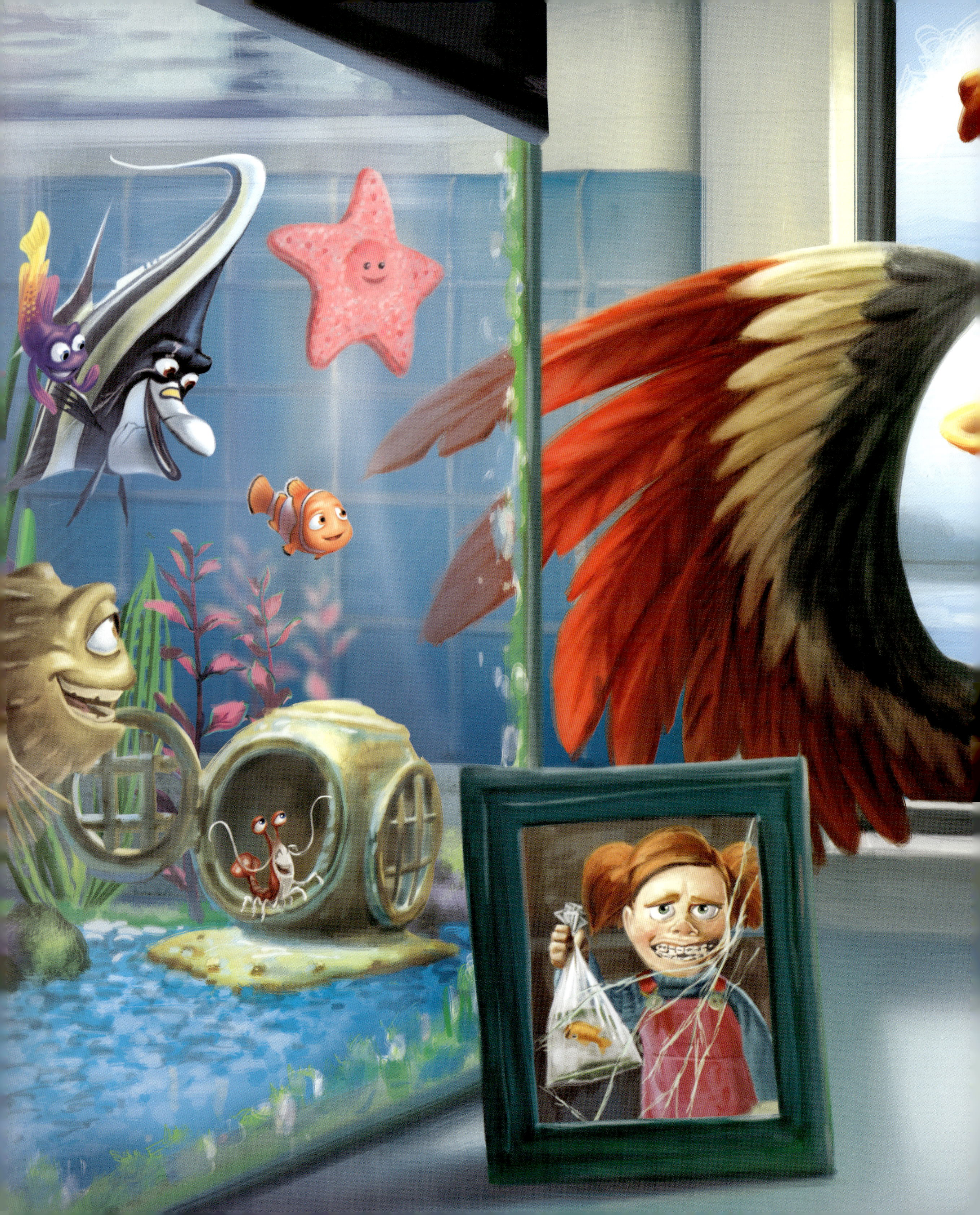

Nemo was determined to escape and find his dad. He darted into the air filter and clogged it up. The tank started filling with green slime.

When the dentist took the fish out of the tank to change the water, they would be able to escape!

Meanwhile, tales of Marlin's rescue mission were spreading far and wide. Nigel the pelican rushed to tell the Tank Gang all about it.

The thought of his dad's bravery filled Nemo with pride.

Out at sea, Marlin and Dory had said goodbye to the turtles only to be swallowed up by a huge whale!

Luckily, the whale was friendly and it soon squirted the two fish out of its blowhole, right into Sydney Harbour!

But their dangerous journey wasn't over yet. A hungry pelican tried to eat Marlin and Dory for breakfast! Thankfully, Nigel came to the rescue. 'Hop inside my mouth if you want to live,' he said.

The next morning, the Tank Gang awoke to find the water clean again. The dentist had fitted a new filter and their plan was ruined!

Worse still, Darla arrived to take Nemo away in a plastic bag....

Suddenly, Nigel flew in through the open window. In the confusion, Nemo got dropped and his plastic bag burst!

Darla tried to grab hold of Nemo, but the little fish quickly jumped into the dentist's sink and escaped down the drain.

Nigel took Marlin and Dory back out to the harbour. Marlin was heartbroken at losing his son yet again.

Meanwhile, Nemo found himself back in the ocean. He bumped into Dory, who remembered she had to reunite Marlin and Nemo at once!

Soon after Marlin and Nemo were together once more. Marlin realized that although Nemo was little, he could do big and brave things!

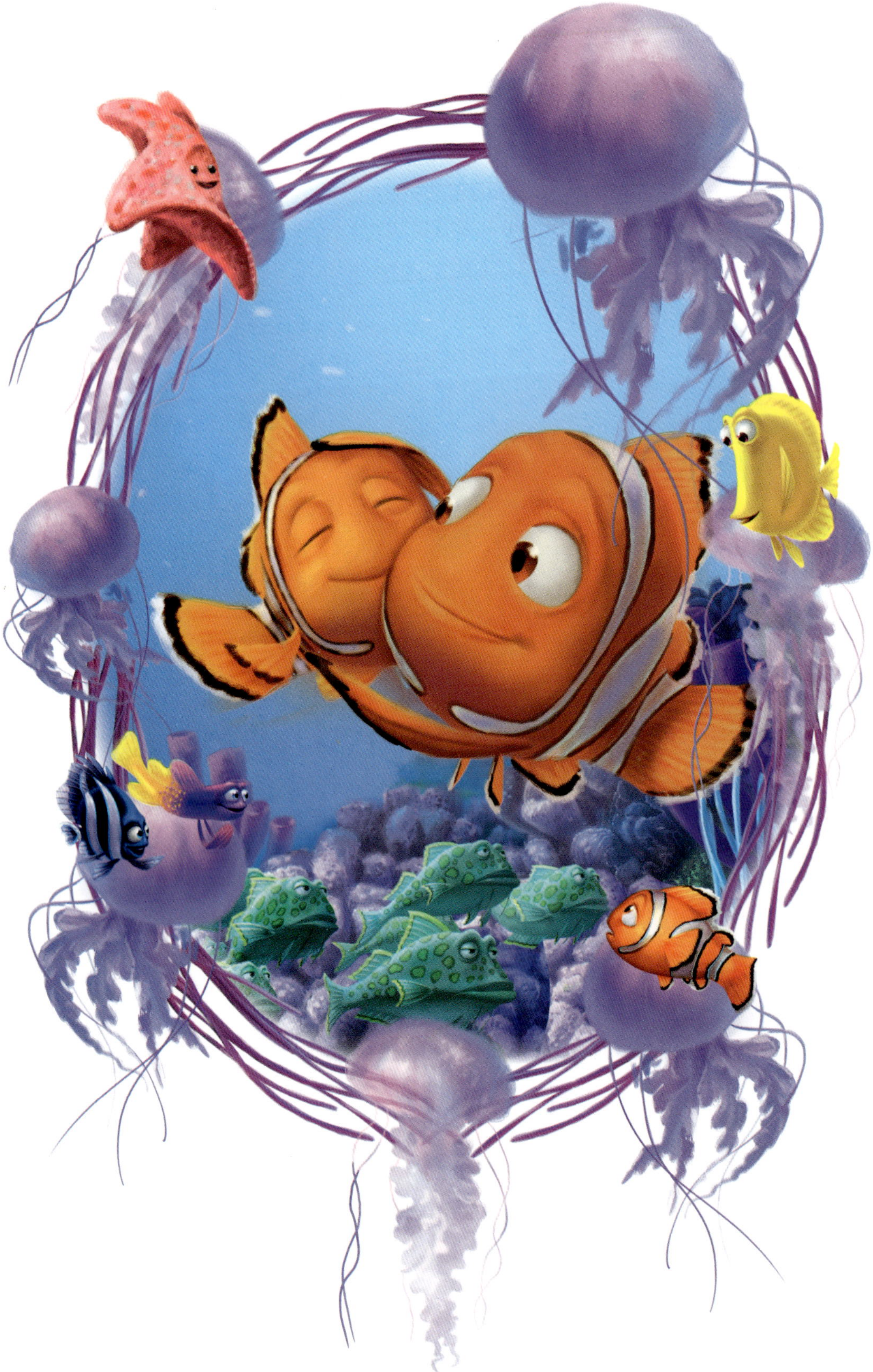